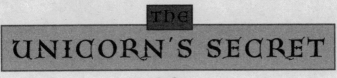

THE UNICORN'S SECRET

#3

The Silver Bracelet

THE UNICORN'S SECRET

#3

The Silver Bracelet

by Kathleen Duey
illustrated by Omar Rayyan

ALADDIN PAPERBACKS

New York London Toronto Sydney Singapore

For all the daydreamers . . .

First Aladdin edition April 2002
Text copyright © 2002 by Kathleen Duey
Illustrations copyright © 2002 by Omar Rayyan

Aladdin Paperbacks
An imprint of Simon & Schuster
Children's Publishing Division
1230 Avenue of the Americas
New York, NY 10020

Also available in an Aladdin library edition.
Designed by Debra Sfetsios
The text of this book was set in Golden Cockerel ITC.
Printed in the United States of America
4 6 8 10 9 7 5

ISBN: 0-689-84271-6
The Library of Congress Control Number for Paperback Edition: 2001097964

Winter is nearly over. Heart is glad—but she is also afraid. Will Tin Blackaby's men start searching for her again? Ruth Oakes, Ash Grove's healer, is the only one who knows where Heart is hiding. She brings Heart food. She gave her leather boots and a thick felt coat. Heart knows she can't hide in her cave forever. But where can she go?

Where will the unicorns be safe?

✦

✦ CHAPTER ONE

Heart stood behind the lightning-split pine tree, waiting.

It was cold.

She envied Moonsilver and Avamir, still warm and asleep back in the cave. Kip would be curled up between them, warmest of all.

"Please be careful, Ruth," she whispered.

Little clouds of her breath hung in the air.

Heart rubbed her mittened hands together.

Somewhere above her on the mountainside, she heard a quail waking, piping sleepily.

Heart was nervous even though they had been very careful. Sometimes Ruth came in the evening, sometimes in the morning.

Sometimes the visits were ten days apart.

Sometimes five or seven or twelve.

They never met in the same place twice.

Ruth always went to visit a patient first. She checked on a number of older people farther out on the Derrytown road. She met with Heart on her way back to Ash Grove.

So far, it had worked.

Tin Blackaby's men were used to Ruth coming and going to tend to the sick. There had always been baskets of apples and bags of wheat in her wagon. Her patients paid her with whatever they had.

Heart sighed and glanced out at the empty road.

They had worked out a signal. If Ruth wore her red hat, it meant she had seen someone on the road. Her blue hat meant everything was safe.

The red hat warned Heart to stay hidden, that Ruth wouldn't slow—or even glance at her—as she passed.

Ruth had worn her red hat only twice. The

first time, Tin Blackaby's men had been following her. The second time it had just been a farmer's wagon.

Heart rubbed her hands together harder, trying to keep them warm.

Finally she heard a faint clopping sound and held her breath as it got louder. She peeked out from behind the tree and grinned. Ruth was wearing her blue hat, pulled low over her ears.

As the wagon came closer, Heart stepped forward just far enough for Ruth to spot her.

"Whoa, Banjo," Ruth called to her bay gelding. She pulled him to a stop, then sat, looking straight ahead. "Hello, dear girl," she said without turning.

"Hello," Heart whispered back.

Ruth got down from the wagon and walked around to lift the bay's rear hoof.

She always did this when she and Heart met.

In case someone came up the road it would look as if Ruth had stopped to see if her horse had picked up a stone.

3

"You are well?" Ruth asked, using a stick to clean Banjo's hoof.

"I am," Heart assured her. "Kip is still catching rabbits almost every day. Avamir and Moonsilver are finding enough grass." Heart stepped forward. "How are you?"

Ruth let go of the bay's hoof. She fiddled with the harness, her back to Heart. "I can outwork any mule I ever met."

Heart smiled. "Have the rumors died down?"

Ruth shrugged. "The man who thought Moonsilver was a goat is still boasting about what fools the others are. Simon still claims you stole *his* horses."

"But have the unicorn rumors stopped?" Heart asked.

Ruth shrugged again. "No. Everyone loves the old stories too much. But people laugh. No one really *believes* there was a unicorn in Ash Grove."

Heart sighed. It was the best she could hope for. "Will you hide the wagon and come up to the cave with me?" Heart asked. She wanted Ruth to stay.

"Better not," Ruth said. "I am expected back to tend Tibbs Renner's twisted ankle."

Heart frowned. Tibbs had always been mean to her, but she pitied him and understood him. The children of Ash Grove made fun of them both.

"He's being apprenticed in Derrytown," Ruth said. "Wants to learn blacksmithing, his mother says. I suspect he just wants to get away from that cruel father of his."

Ruth walked around her horse, her fingers going through the motions of harness checking. "Simon has been ill."

Heart gasped. "He has?"

"Oh, he will soon recover," Ruth told her. "I made him pay me this time, though."

Heart covered her mouth with one hand. "He *paid* you?"

"Yes," Ruth said. She glanced up the road, then back toward Ash Grove. "With these." She pulled a little woven bag out of her coat pocket.

She tossed it to Heart, meeting her eyes for an instant. "Simon said they're from the blanket you were wrapped in when he found you. They're silver threads like the one my grandmother gave me. You still have it?"

Heart nodded. "Of course."

"It hurt Simon to give these up," Ruth said.

Heart pressed her lips together. She slipped the little bag into her pocket. "Poor Simon."

Ruth nodded. "Poor indeed. He does not have a single friend."

Heart wiped her eyes.

"Don't pity him too much, Heart," Ruth said. "If he had known for an instant that Moonsilver and Avamir were unicorns—"

"He'd have sold them to Tin Blackaby—or even Lord Dunraven," Heart finished for her.

Ruth nodded. "Even knowing it would break your heart." She looked up the road again, then down it.

Ruth shook her head. Then, swiftly, she

pulled three cloth sacks out of the back of the wagon. She tossed them neatly into the trees.

Heart saw a little tin of cheese roll out the top of one of the sacks and her mouth watered.

"Thank you so much, Ruth," she said quietly.

Ruth looked straight at her for just a moment. "It worries me to death, you being out here alone."

Heart blinked back tears. Ruth smiled at her and walked back around the wagon. She kicked at the narrow iron footrest to knock the snow and mud off her boots. Then she climbed up.

"I will repay you for all this," Heart said.

Ruth made a quiet sound of dismissal. "There is nothing to repay. I just wish I could make things right, that's all."

Heart sighed. "Be careful, please. Tin Blackaby might—"

"No, he won't hurt me," Ruth interrupted her. "I tend to him, same as everyone else."

Heart nodded, knowing that Ruth couldn't see her. She was looking straight ahead again.

"Let's meet in five days, by the white boulder on the straightaway before this one," Ruth said. "Come at noon."

Heart knew the flat-topped white rock that stood near the road. "I will be waiting," she said. "Thank you, Ruth."

Ruth glanced at her. Heart felt the look like a warm touch.

A single instant after that, Heart heard the thudding of hooves on the snow-packed road.

Someone was coming fast and riding hard.

CHAPTER TWO

"Ruth!" Heart whispered. The hoofbeats were getting louder.

"Take care, little one," Ruth answered quietly. She shook the reins hard.

Banjo lurched into a gallop.

Heart ducked back into the trees.

Just then, Tin Blackaby's men burst around the bend, their horses galloping. They saw Ruth's wagon and reined in, surrounding her.

Heart watched through the tree branches, her breath uneven. She couldn't hear what they were saying.

Suddenly Ruth jumped down from the driver's bench. She came striding back, then faced the men, her hands on her hips. She looked furious.

"I dropped my coin purse when your horses startled mine," she accused. She walked toward Heart, staring down at the mud and ice in the road.

Heart crouched, hiding.

"I meant to see my patient again in five days," Ruth shouted angrily at the men. "Why do I have to wait two weeks?"

One of the men spurred his horse toward Ruth. "It's Blackaby's decree, Healer. "

"Why is he closing the road?" Ruth asked, pretending to grab something from the ground, then walking toward the rider.

"He hasn't told us anything," the man growled.

Heart watched Ruth get into her wagon. The riders trotted alongside as Banjo started off.

Heart stood still until they were out of sight.

Ruth had found a way to make sure Heart understood what had happened. Heart was grateful. But she was still worried.

She gathered the supplies Ruth had brought, then started uphill, tears in her eyes.

As she walked into the cave, Kip opened his blue eye, then his brown one. He wriggled his way out from between the unicorns.

Moonsilver lifted his head. Avamir scrambled upright.

"Something terrible happened," Heart said aloud, talking to the animals the way she always did. "Tin Blackaby's men came."

She set the food down, then reached into her pocket for the little woven bag Ruth had given her.

She opened it carefully.

There were two long silver threads inside. She passed them between her fingers. They were round and silken.

Heart pulled the tiny pouch Ruth had given her months before from her carry-sack. It held the single silver thread Ruth's grandmother had passed down to her. Heart placed it with the two new threads, then carefully closed the little woven bag.

Heart smiled. Ruth's grandmother had given

her the single silver thread as a luck-charm. Ruth had told Heart it would protect her, too.

Heart sighed.

It had . . . until now.

But how odd that her own mother—whoever she was—had owned a blanket embroidered with thread just like the thread Ruth's grandmother had handed down.

And where was the shop that held such wondrous things?

In Derrytown?

In the village at the foot of Dunraven's castle?

People said these places were full of wonders. Why not a shop that sold silver embroidery thread?

Kip barked softly. Heart turned. "You want your bone?" He barked again.

Heart began to go through the supplies.

As always, Ruth had packed a few surprises. The tinned cheese was for her. She gave Kip his bone. There was corn and oats for the unicorns.

Heart gave them a little of each, then tucked the rest away.

Heart swept the night's ashes aside, then laid kindling on the glowing coals.

Within minutes she had a cook fire to boil her barley.

She ate half as much as she usually would. If Ruth couldn't come for two weeks—or longer— she would need to stretch the food.

Heart cleaned up then walked outside. Kip followed, leaving his bone behind. The unicorns came out a moment later.

Heart looked up at the sky. The worst of the winter storms were over.

Kip leaped into his morning run. He had grown—his legs were getting long. He tore along, circling her.

Moonsilver danced into a canter to play with Kip.

Usually it made Heart smile to watch them. Today she just sighed and leaned against Avamir.

"This is awful," she said aloud. "I don't want to cause trouble for Ruth."

She knew she should leave.

But where could she possibly go?

✦ CHAPTER THREE

The next morning, Heart heard voices. Picking her way downhill, staying hidden, she saw Tin Blackaby's men pass on the road. The following afternoon, they passed by again.

Were they looking for *her*?

Would they look this hard for two horses and a ragged girl? It seemed impossible. Unless they suspected the truth about Moonsilver and Avamir

The idea they might know about the unicorns made Heart's throat ache.

"It doesn't matter," Heart told Kip the next day as they sat beside a snowy meadow.

Moonsilver and Avamir were grazing above them, pawing at the snow to uncover the frozen grass.

Kip tilted his head and stared at her.

"It doesn't matter why they are searching," Heart went on. "If they keep at it, we'll have to leave."

The next day, Heart watched the road.

She saw no one at all.

The morning after that, her spirits lifted a little. She found herself hoping.

Maybe Ruth would come to the white-rock meeting place after all. Maybe she would explain that Tin Blackaby had been upset about something else, that it had nothing to do with her or Heart or the unicorns.

Heart started up to the meadow.

As always, she led the unicorns and Kip across the rockiest ground she could find.

They left no tracks among the rocks.

It was safe. The unicorns *never* stumbled.

Kip was as surefooted as any dog.

Heart was the one who had to be careful on the rough ground.

The rising sun made the snow sparkle.

Kip played with a stick for a while. Then Heart made snowballs, throwing them for him to chase.

She watched Kip bounding through the snow. Each time she threw a snowball he raced back to drop it near her feet.

"Kip?" Heart said. He stopped looked up at her, his ears high. "We have to leave here."

Kip's ears went down. Heart knew he could hear the worry in her voice.

Heart closed her eyes, scared even to think about it.

They would have to travel on the road. The snow was too deep on the slopes; they could get lost too easily. But if they stayed in the cave and were found . . .

By early evening, Heart was tired of worrying.

"Suppertime," she said. Kip shook snow from his coat.

"Avamir?" Heart called. "Moonsilver?"

The unicorns stopped grazing to look at her.

"Let's go home," Heart called to them. They

turned and began to pick their way through the deep snow toward the rocks.

Once the fire had warmed the cave a little, Heart poured out a little barley to boil.

"You catch rabbits, Kip," she said. "The unicorns graze. I'm the only one who needs Ruth's help all the time."

Kip tilted his head. Then his ears jerked upward. He faced the cave entrance.

Heart scrambled to her feet. "What?"

Kip whimpered. He lifted one forepaw. Then he growled low in his throat.

Heart heard something faint, far away.

Voices?

✦ CHAPTER FOUR

"Kip!"

He looked up at her.

"Stay there!" Heart said.

She ran to the entrance. When she peeked out, she saw people coming out of the trees at the far end of the meadow.

They were dressed in bright colors. Some led ponies. And as they walked, they *jingled*.

Gypsies?

Heart ducked back inside.

She had heard about Gypsies all her life. But they rarely passed through Ash Grove. Why would they? Tin Blackaby wouldn't pay for their shows and the villagers had no money to spare.

Heart inched forward to peek outside again.

Some of the women wore long, swirling skirts. Some had wide, billowing trousers like the men's. The men's sleeves were gathered and full. All of them—even the toddling babies— wore wide sashes that dangled rainbows of silk tassels.

Heart watched them come up the slope in a ragged line. They were heading straight toward her. They were carrying bedrolls and blankets. Heart's stomach tightened as she realized that her cave was *their* cave. And they intended to shelter in it for the night.

Heart knew one thing.

She couldn't let them see Moonsilver.

"Stay inside, Avamir," Heart pleaded. The mare shook her mane and tossed her head. "Keep Moonsilver with you too," Heart added, then stared at the colt. He switched his long tail back and forth.

Heart took a deep breath.

If she waited any longer the Gypsies would be

too close. She stepped out of the cave into the late afternoon sunlight.

The Gypsies stopped, hands on hips, glancing at each other. Heart's pulse was a quick-time hammer.

Would they hurt her?

Heart stood still, her breath uneven. Suddenly, the Gypsies walked back downslope. They picked a place in the meadow to set up camp.

Heart stepped back into the cave entrance, then watched.

The Gypsy women made a fire—a big fire. They stood around, talking. Bursts of laughter came from the children.

The sun was setting.

It'd be dark soon.

Heart clenched her teeth.

She had been so careful with her cooking fires. And now these Gypsies had built a bonfire anyone could see.

"Wait here," she told to Avamir and Moonsilver.

"You have to stay hidden." She looked at Kip. "Don't follow me."

Kip tilted his head and whined, which meant he had understood and didn't like it one bit.

Heart started down the slope, her feet heavy as lead.

One of the Gypsy children looked up. "She's come out!"

All the Gypsies turned to look up the slope.

Heart slowed. Many of them were smiling at her. It surprised her. They didn't look angry about her using their cave at all.

"We were going to ask you if we could at least bed down inside," the boy shouted.

"Hush, Davey," an old man said to him.

Davey grinned. "Zim thought it'd be best to bring you a bowl of stew to bargain with." He gestured toward the old man.

The instant he said it, Heart smelled the deep, wonderful aroma of a real supper cooking.

"We've got grand biscuits, too," a merry-faced girl called. Davey smiled. "That's Fiona. She made the biscuits."

Heart blinked as the Gypsies laughed. She had never, in her whole life, been around so many friendly people.

"Where are your folks?" Davey asked. "Where are you from?"

She looked at him. "Ash Grove. But I don't have any folks."

One of the older women made a clucking sound of dismay. "None? You can't be out here by yourself, can you, dearie?"

Heart backed up a step, sorry she had spoken. She couldn't explain herself to these people. And if they saw the unicorns . . .

"You could come with us, then," Davey said.

There was a general sound of agreement. The old woman who had called her "dearie" was nodding. "Do you juggle? Can you dance?"

Heart shook her head, confused.

"I'll teach her," Davey said. "Look how little her feet are. She'd be a perfect doll up there."

Heart stared at him. Up where? She had no idea what he was talking about.

"You'll need an act of some kind," the older woman said.

A man across the fire nodded. "A little thing like you can do most anything and people will applaud. But you'll grow. So it's best to learn something and—"

He stopped suddenly and stared past her. Heart turned to see Kip racing down the hill.

"Kip!" she shouted. "Stop right there!"

Kip slid to a stop and sat down, tilting his head.

A murmuring went around the fire.

"Has a touch with animals, don't she?" the man said, and laughed.

Heart sighed.

The fire was warm and they were all smiling at her.

She smiled back, wishing she belonged to them.

"Will you look at that!" one of the men said in a low voice.

He was pointing.

Heart turned back toward the cave.

Avamir was standing in the opening, peering out. And beside her was Moonsilver. His horn glistened in the dusk.

✦ CHAPTER FIVE

Everyone was staring, talking in excited voices.

"You clever child," the older woman said, coming around the bonfire to look into Heart's face. "We've heard the tales, of course. Some guard claims he saw a unicorn?"

Heart swallowed hard, confused and uncertain what to say.

"I'm Binney," the woman said, smiling. "That one named me." She pointed at Davey.

"She's my Granny Binnadell," he explained. "When I was little, I couldn't say it right."

"So he called me Binney and Binney I became," the woman added. She faced Heart. "Now, tell us how you did it."

"Please," Davey added.

Heart glanced at him, her pulse speeding up.

"Pine gum to stick it on?" Davey asked. "What is it, a goat horn?"

"Whatever it is, we should have thought it up," Heart heard a man mutter. "Folks are going to line up to see this."

All at once, Heart understood.

The Gypsies thought Moonsilver was a colt with an old goat horn stuck on his forehead with sticky tree sap. They thought she had done it to make money.

Heart exhaled loudly. Then she cleared her throat. "Well, he's white, like all the legends say, and . . . so I . . ." Heart trailed off.

She was not used to lying.

Binney laughed, lifting her eyes to the dusky sky. "Rumors also say a little girl stole the horses. Did you?"

Heart straightened her spine. "I *paid* Simon. He lied. And I—"

"That's plenty." Binney waved one hand in the air. "I can hear the truth in your voice. The rest is your business." She gestured up at Moonsilver. "Jacob is right. People will line up. You are very clever."

Heart let out a slow, careful breath.

Binney looked at her, dark eyes steady. "Why you're alone is your business, so long as your troubles bring us no harm."

Heart told the truth. "Tin Blackaby's men might be searching for me."

Binney nodded slowly. "People look for us, too, sometimes." Everyone laughed. Binney hushed them. "Do you want to be found?"

Heart shook her head.

"Will they follow you to Derrytown and beyond?" Binney's eyes were sharp.

Heart thought about it.

Beyond Derrytown?

Tin Blackaby's men never even rode all the way *to* Derrytown. No one from Ash Grove went that far.

"No," she answered.

"What's your name?" Binney asked.

Heart told her.

"Then join us, Heart, do," Binney said. "We're off to Derrytown with many stops in between here and there. Then on to Yolen's Crossing and San Coville and—what?" she asked, peering into Heart's face.

"I've never heard of those places," Heart said quietly.

Binney laughed again. "Nor have the people there heard of your little thatched-roof Ash Grove. If you go far enough, you will find people who haven't heard of your Lord Dunraven."

Heart caught her breath. "Is that true?"

Binney nodded, her eyes twinkling.

Heart smiled. Then her eyes flooded with tears. Maybe she'd never see Ruth again.

Zim pointed to Kip. "How well is he trained?"

Heart realized Kip was wagging his tail, staring at her.

"He's smart," Heart said. "I've never taught him tricks."

"Call him," Zim said quietly.

"Kip?" Heart said. "Will you come down here?" She heard the Gypsy children giggling.

Kip lunged into a headlong run. Sliding on the snowy patches, he charged down the slope. He skidded to a stop beside Heart.

"There's a dog that knows good biscuits when he smells them," Fiona said.

Everyone laughed again.

Heart let the sound wash over her. Ruth would love these people, she was sure.

Heart glanced back at the cave entrance. The dusk was deepening. Moonsilver and Avamir had gone back inside.

Zim ladled stew into a bowl. Then he scooped in clean snow to cool it.

"Tell him not to eat it," he said to Heart.

"Why?" She frowned, puzzled.

"To see if he really listens to you."

"Kip," Heart said somberly as Zim set the bowl in front of him. "Don't touch it, please." Kip looked sad, but he didn't move.

The Gypsies stared, then applauded.

"You have the gift," Zim said approvingly. He caught Heart's eye. "Tell him it's his."

"You can eat it, Kip," she said quietly.

Kip buried his muzzle in the bowl, lapping noisily.

"Are the horses trained like this?" Zim asked her.

Heart shrugged. "The . . . horses are smart too. Moonsilver is shy—"

"The colt?" Zim interrupted.

Heart nodded.

"I'm surprised he stands for the spirit gum and the goat horn."

Heart hoped he couldn't see her blushing in the soft dusk. "I mean, he's shy with everyone but me," she explained.

"Would it be all right with him if we slept inside the cave, do you think?" Davey asked. He shivered and grinned.

Heart glanced around at the eager faces. It was getting chilly. Binney was ladling stew and Heart knew it was for her.

"Of course," she said slowly.

Zim pulled a silver flute from beneath his coat. He began to play. The melody was like rainwater, quick and clear.

Heart stared at his fingers. The firelight polished the silver flute into gold.

"Do you play?" Zim asked, when he finished the tune.

Heart shook her head.

"I will teach you if you like."

Heart nodded, smiling. She ate fast.

The Gypsies were standing, stretching. They were gathering their blankets and carry-sacks.

It was nearly dark as they trudged up the hill behind Heart.

She was grateful.

The unicorns came to the entrance when they heard the voices. Avamir led Moonsilver to stand in the meadow while the Gypsies settled in for the night.

Heart moved her things to the front of the cave.

It was strange to hear so many voices inside it.

One by one they quieted, calling good night to her.

Only when it was silent did the unicorns come back to the cave.

She waited until they had lain down just inside the entrance. Kip curled up between them.

Then, being as quiet as she could, Heart went through went her carry-sack. She finally found the empty cheese tin.

She placed it beside her blankets and lay down to wait.

She bit at her lip to keep from falling asleep.

She had to wait for the moon to rise.

And she had to be careful.

If even one of the Gypsies heard her leave the cave, it would ruin everything.

CHAPTER SIX

When the moon finally came up, Heart tiptoed out so quietly that even Kip did not waken.

She used clean snow to scrub out the little cheese tin. Then she made her way, shivering, to the edge of the woods.

Working in the pale light, she found a thick gob of pinesap oozing from a limb low enough to reach.

She scraped it into the tin.

Back in the cave, she held the closed tin against her belly to warm it.

When the pine gum was softened, she gently wakened Moonsilver.

"Hold still," she begged him. "Hush."

She smeared a circle of the sticky pine gum

around the base of his horn.

Then she lightly kissed his muzzle and put the tin away.

She managed to doze a little, but she dreamed that she was running uphill. She woke up breathing hard, as though the steep rocky hillside of her dream had been real.

She lay still, until the Gypsies rose at daybreak. Then she got up.

The unicorns moved away to the meadow, pawing up grass to eat.

Heart thought the tree gum looked perfect. No one else seemed to notice.

The Gypsies sang as they broke camp. The bells on their sashes jingled. The children chased each other, laughing.

Heart packed her carry-sack. It did not take long. All of her possessions fit inside.

Kip stood close to her as the Gypsies left the cave.

The children stared wide-eyed at Moonsilver, giggling.

Binney and Zim smiled broadly.

"Do you need help?" Fiona asked on her way past Heart. Davey was right behind her. Heart shook her head, and they went on.

"Moonsilver was a baby when we found this place," Heart whispered to Avamir once they were alone. "Now he's nearly as tall as you are."

Avamir's breath smelled like sweet grass.

"I'm afraid," Heart said softly.

Avamir nudged her shoulder, then whinnied softly at Moonsilver.

Heart watched the colt canter up, then slide to a halt. She laughed. "You two aren't scared, are you?" She took Ruth's little woven bag from her pocket and opened it to touch the silver threads.

Heart caught her breath.

Simon's threads had knotted themselves into a circle with Ruth's. *How?*

"Heart!"

Davey's shout made her whirl around. She pushed the silvery circle back inside the woven bag.

She started down the mountain, Kip at her heels.

Avamir followed. Moonsilver cantered in a wide arc, then caught up. Heart wondered what the Gypsies would think. The unicorns never had on a rope or a halter.

She wouldn't be able to make them act like horses.

Maybe the Gypsies would think she had trained them.

Heart could hear Gypsies singing and talking. They had hidden their wagons in the trees. They were moving them back onto the road now.

Heart took a deep breath and stepped out of the forest.

The unicorns were right behind her.

Sighs and murmurs rose from the Gypsies.

Moonsilver *was* beautiful, even with the sticky ring of pinesap on his snowy white forehead. Avamir was stately, like a queen in a story. Both were more graceful than any horse ever born.

Heart was uneasy standing out in the open. She was used to *hiding*. What if Tin Blackaby's men came galloping up? Glancing around, she recognized a flat-topped white boulder.

Heart sighed. This was where she was supposed to meet Ruth next time.

Avamir and Moonsilver drifted back into the trees. They began to paw at the snow.

Kip ran to meet a small, black dog tagging after Fiona.

"Sadie won't fight," Fiona called. "We'll all watch out for Kip."

"Heart?"

She turned. Davey was pointing at the unicorns. "Binney wondered—don't they just wander off?"

Heart shook her head. "Never."

Davey's smiled. "That horn looks amazing from a distance. Maybe you won't need to learn to wire walk." He waved and went back to help the men who were rolling wagons back onto the road.

The sun was coming up.

It made the wagons shine. Each was painted differently, with bright patterns sweeping along its sides. Binney's was meadow-flower blue.

Heart watched the laughing Gypsies, her own spirits sinking lower and lower. Ruth would look for her. Then she would worry.

Heart watched a girl her age standing on a box to fasten harness buckles.

Some of the children were gathering pinecones.

Older ones brought buckets of icy creek water to fill the oaken barrels on the wagons.

Heart saw a glimmer of silver in the frozen mud.

It was a tiny Gypsy bell, fallen from someone's sash.

She scooped it up, smiling. Maybe there *was* a way to let Ruth know she was with the Gypsies.

Heart took the circle of silver thread out of its woven bag and put it on her wrist, like a bracelet.

Then she put the bell in Ruth's little woven bag.

She found a stone the size of a supper plate and pried it loose from the frozen ground.

Glancing around, she made sure no one was watching her.

Then she placed the little bag on the white boulder and hid it with the smaller rock.

Heart glanced around again.

No one had seen her.

She walked back toward the wagons.

✦ CHAPTER SEVEN

The next day, Zim walked beside Heart. He played his silvery flute.

The melodies were like waterfalls, like quick-winged birds flying through a forest.

That evening Zim taught Heart a simple scale. He lent her a flute so she could practice. She had to slide the circle of silver thread higher on her arm or it would get in her way. She didn't take it off. She never wanted to lose it.

Once she had learned the first scale, Zim taught her another. The silvery flute felt cool and smooth beneath Heart's fingers.

Every night, Heart slept in Binney's warm, clean wagon. It smelled like herbs and apples, and she felt safe inside it. Binney gave her a soft blanket and a pillow. Binney's heart was clear as creek water. She was like Ruth.

Every morning, Binney's blue wagon led the way. The other drivers followed in a long line.

As they wound their way down out of the mountains, the weather warmed. Soon there was no snow on the ground at all.

Dozens of roads crossed the Derrytown road. The Gypsies knew which ones to take.

Heart was happy—and *busy*. There were enough hands for every chore—and enough work to keep all hands moving.

Every morning, the Gypsies folded their blankets, shook out their pillows, and made breakfast. They tended their babies, washed their children's faces, and fed their dogs.

They left nothing behind but boot prints.

Every evening, away from the wagons where no one could see, Heart redrew the sticky pinegum circle on Moonsilver's forehead.

He did not seem to mind.

The unicorns slept near Binney's wagon. The

Gypsies admired them, but no one tried to touch them.

Heart was grateful. Moonsilver's secret had to be kept.

At first Heart walked with Kip, Avamir, and Moonsilver. Then things began to change.

Kip often visited Sadie, Fiona's dog.

Sometimes Heart joined Binney or Fiona and her friends.

She showed them how to pick and dry meadowsweet and how to make the healing salve Ruth had used on Moonsilver's wound back in Ash Grove.

Zim walked beside Heart to teach her the scales. She carried the flute and practiced each day.

Davey sometimes walked where he could watch the unicorns. Avamir was friendly with the children, but Moonsilver remained shy. Heart was glad. She didn't want anyone to realize his horn was real.

In the camps at night Heart learned what

Davey had meant by wirewalking and juggling.

The Gypsies tied wires between two trees. One was low so the children could practice. The higher one was for the adults.

It looked impossible.

How could anyone balance?

Heart was afraid to try it.

"Have you planned your act yet?" Binney asked gently, almost every day.

"No," Heart answered every time.

Binney would smile. "It will come to you."

"Everyone is so good," Heart said to Davey one evening as they watched the wirewalkers.

He glanced at her. "Of course. We practice hard."

Heart thought about it as she snuggled into her soft blanket inside Binney's wagon that night.

The next day she started playing the flute every moment she could.

"You are ready," Zim said a few days later. He showed her a song. It was harder than the scales.

Heart practiced. Once she could play the song, she found herself adding notes to make it prettier.

Then she made up a song of her own.

Kip loved it.

He came running whenever she played it.

Zim grinned. He told her to give Kip a bit of bread every time he came to hear the tune.

Heart did. Soon Kip leaped into a mad dash the instant he heard the first few notes. Moonsilver noticed. He began to follow Kip.

It became a race between them.

They would slide to a stop in front of Heart.

Then Moonsilver would go back to graze with Avamir.

Kip would wander through the wagons.

He played with all the dogs, but Sadie adored him. He followed Binney asking for leftover stew.

They came to a village named Fallbrook. It was small, its hills covered with fruit trees and farms.

It's prettier than Ash Grove, Heart thought. The people had better houses.

Heart walked close to the unicorns. They seemed calm—much calmer than she was.

"We'd like to show Moonsilver tonight," Binney said. "Have you planned an act?"

Heart shook her head, blushing.

Binney patted Heart's cheek. "Let us do it, then. You can change it later to suit yourself." She touched Heart's arm. "Look."

Heart glanced around.

People had stopped. They were staring at Moonsilver.

✦ CHAPTER EIGHT

Binney raised her hand and signaled.

The Gypsies pulled in their ponies.

Zim jumped down to play his flute. He gestured for Heart to join in. She pushed the silver thread-bracelet higher on her arm and lifted the flute. She played as well as she could.

The Gypsy children appeared in a long, laughing line.

They turned flips and danced.

They shouted to the people they passed, inviting them to a show in a few hours.

"Tell your neighbors!" Binney shouted. "Come to see Dunraven's Rumor—a real unicorn!"

People waved and called back, laughing.

Binney gestured, and the wagons creaked back into motion.

Heart felt breathless. The Gypsy wagons followed a cobbled road to a meadow at the edge of the town.

Avamir and Moonsilver walked a little ways off to graze on the fresh spring grass. Kip stayed close to them.

Heart fidgeted when Lord Dunraven's steward came to talk to Binney. But he was a jolly-faced man—nothing like Tin Blackaby.

He joked with Binney.

His eyes went wide when he noticed Moonsilver.

Heart's breath stopped in her throat.

"Now that's clever," the man remarked.

Binney was counting coins into his hand. She smiled. "You've heard the tales?"

He shrugged. "Some wheat-gleaner in a thatch-roofed village claiming he saw a herd of unicorns in Dunraven's forest?" He chuckled. "Who hasn't? But people will get a smile out of this."

Binney half bowed. "That is our trade. We sell smiles."

The man laughed. "I'll bring my family to the show."

Binney made him a curtsy as he left. "He takes a big share, but they all do," she said wearily. "At least he's more pleasant than most. That's why his town does well."

Heart was trembling. Maybe this was foolish. What if someone guessed Moonsilver really was a unicorn?

"You're shaking like a leaf in high wind," Binney said gently. She nudged Heart's shoulder. "Go. Get ready."

The Gypsies' everyday clothes were colorful. Their costumes were embroidered, trimmed, mirrored, and beaded.

Heart was dazzled.

Fiona loaned her a loose-sleeved raspberry blouse and an embroidered pinafore of columbine blue.

Talia's aunt gave her a copper-colored scarf

with a lacey edge. Josepha smiled and clapped. Heart felt beautiful.

When people began to arrive at dusk, Binney told her to hide Moonsilver behind the wagons. "And put this in your pocket." She handed Heart bits of bread.

Heart helped set out the circle of Gypsy lanterns.

The meadow became a magical place.

The jugglers began the show.

Davey was amazing. He juggled heavy clubs, then balls, then sticks that had been set on fire! Two grown men juggled with him. They threw balls between them, their hands flashing.

Then came the wirewalkers.

The wire was strung high, between two elm trees.

The girls did graceful tricks. One of them did a slow somersault, gripping the wire in her hands, then coming back up onto her feet.

The crowd clapped and shouted.

Heart clapped with them, staring.

Then Davey walked the wire. Heart blinked. She had never even seen him practice! He pretended to fall, but caught the wire and swung around it, then stood up again.

The crowd gasped, then clapped.

While they were still clapping, Binney danced forward on the grass. She wore a sparkling gold skirt. She put a flaming torch into her mouth, then breathed out a long plume of fire.

The audience fell silent.

Binney breathed out fire like a dragon in a bedtime tale.

Then, from somewhere in the dark, Zim began to play. After a moment, he stepped into the lantern circle. The light sparkled off his flute.

He played a melody that made Heart's skin prickle.

The people clapped and whistled.

Then Binney walked out again. "We have something very special tonight," she said. "A girl who plays a magic flute."

The people applauded.

Heart stood still, trembling.

She felt Davey pressing her flute into her hand. "Go on," he whispered in her ear. "You'll be wonderful."

Heart managed to walk forward and bow.

"She plays many melodies," Binney was saying. "But there is one tune that sometimes calls up magical beasts!"

Binney bowed to the audience, then backed out of the light.

Heart touched her pocket. The bread was there. She took a deep breath.

Heart began to play. Her breathing was a little uneven, but the tune sounded all right.

The second song was better. She danced a little. People clapped. For the third song, she played Kip's melody.

As he had dozens of times before, Kip came running the instant he heard the first notes.

Moonsilver was right behind him. They raced in a long circle, Moonsilver leaping and tossing his head.

Heart stood with her head high, her back straight.

She kept playing as Kip and Moonsilver plunged to a stop in front of her.

The melody whirled and spun across the soft evening air.

The people stared at Moonsilver. They stared at Kip. Only then did Heart notice a ruff of false hair around Kip's neck. Someone had gummed a tuft on the end of his tail, too.

He looked like a tiny, patchy-coated lion.

She saw Davey grinning from beyond the lanterns.

Moonsilver pawed the ground. Kip ran in a tight circle around him. The audience roared its approval.

The noise startled Moonsilver into another headlong gallop.

He circled the whole meadow, tossing his head. His snow-white coat gleamed in the lantern light.

Coming back, Kip crossed in front of

Moonsilver. The colt leaped over him, landing as lightly as a cat.

The audience stood and cheered.

Moonsilver reared, pawing at the summer night.

"They just think you are beautiful," Heart said to him, lowering the flute. "Don't be afraid."

Moonsilver calmed down. He stood on all four hooves and tossed his head. Then he bent to rub his muzzle on one foreleg.

It looked like he was bowing.

The audience clapped and cheered again. They applauded for a long time.

The show was over, and Binney told them good night.

It took a long time for them to leave. Heart stood beside Moonsilver, waving good-bye, smiling and smiling.

"You were wonderful," Binney told her the next morning. "You made them happy."

Davey was standing nearby. He turned and nodded. "They'll talk about that for months."

Moonsilver tossed his head.

"You were wonderful too," Davey assured him.

The colt pricked his ears and listened.

"He likes you," Heart said.

Davey grinned.

✦ CHAPTER NINE

The next show was in a smaller town called Bonsall.

The one after that was in Finley, a town built around a water-wheeled flourmill.

Then came Cusick's Farm, Mayes, Harlan Bend, and Werlinburg.

Heart began to dance more while she played the flute. Fiona taught her steps. She practiced playing. She learned to make each note shine like a star.

Moonsilver seemed to like making people clap and whistle.

Heart taught him signals. If she raised one finger, he would bow. Two fingers made him gallop in a circle. She taught him to rear when she lifted her head and crossed her eyes.

Kip learned fast, too.

Every show got better.

The Gypsies were delighted.

Heart taught Kip to bare his teeth like a lion. It made people laugh aloud.

Fiona helped sometimes. She began to think up new tricks to teach Sadie, too. Fiona—and her friends Talia and Josepha—began to sit next to Heart at the campfire.

Talia and Josepha had a balancing act. They could spin plates on their fingers. They could dance with swords balanced across their foreheads. They practiced nearly every evening.

"Heart! Watch!" Davey called one night in camp.

She turned to see him climbing the ladder to the low wire.

Holding his juggling clubs, he stepped onto the slender line.

Heart stared as he set his feet.

Then he began to juggle. The whole camp went quiet. Heart realized she was holding her breath.

How could he do it? Juggling looked hard enough standing on firm ground.

Davey took a step forward, then another, then a third.

He caught all the clubs, then dropped them so he could raise his hands high and bow.

Everyone cheered and clapped.

Davey leaped down from the low wire, grinning. Heart shook her head as he came toward her. "When have you been practicing that?" she demanded.

Davey shrugged. "After everyone goes to sleep."

Heart frowned. "Why keep it a secret?"

He lowered his head. "In case I couldn't do it. I'll try the high wire next."

Heart shook her head. "But then, if you lose your balance, you'll—"

Davey waved one hand in the air to stop her. "But I won't!"

"No one juggles up there," Heart argued. But Davey's eyes were shining and he only smiled at her.

Seven days later, they came to Derrytown, late at night.

Binney had insisted they travel past dark.

She didn't want the whole town to see Moonsilver before the show.

Derrytown amazed Heart. There were tall posts with lanterns hanging from them on street corners.

The shops were all closed, but there were so many of them!

Everything was sold here.

Maybe she would find a shop that sold silver thread.

"I dreamed of coming here when I first found you in the forest," she whispered to Avamir as they walked.

Then she smiled. She had long ago imagined *riding* into Derrytown on Avamir, wearing fancy boots and a nice coat.

"This is better," she whispered to Avamir. "I am walking next to a dear friend." She turned the silver circle on her wrist, thinking about Ruth.

Kip barked at a cat.

The unicorn mare shook her mane, startled. Heart heard a faint jingling. Heart smiled. One of the Gypsy girls had braided a few tiny bells into Avamir's mane.

The unicorn mare was making new friends, too.

Heart hoped they could stay with the Gypsies forever.

The hanging lanterns made perfect globes of yellow light.

"Have you ever seen a real town?" Davey asked, falling into step beside her.

"No." Heart tilted her head to see the tops of the buildings. Many of them were as tall as a tree. "Do birds nest on the roofs?" she asked Davey.

He narrowed his eyes. "Probably."

"What kind of stone is that?" Heart asked him, touching the rough red surface of the building.

"It's not stone, it's brick," Davey explained. "Made from baked river clay."

Heart touched it again. It *felt* like rock.

They made camp on the level, green meadow in the center of the town square. The steward came to see them, of course. He left with so many coins that Binney spent a few minutes muttering to herself in anger.

Then she cleared her throat and started shouting instructions.

Heart led the unicorns and Kip out of the way.

Binney had the wagoners back into place. The finished circle looked like a spoked wheel.

"There," Binney said wearily, coming to stand by Heart. "We can hide the unicorn inside the circle."

The unicorn.

It made Heart's skin prickle to hear her say it. She settled Moonsilver and Avamir near Binney's wagon for the night. Kip lay down with them.

"How long will we be here?" she asked as she climbed into bed.

"A day or two, no more," Binney told Heart as

they settled down. "Then we'll go on."

"I still can't believe there is anyplace beyond Derrytown," Heart told her.

Binney chuckled. "Oh, there is. You'll see. Remember what I said about people not knowing your Lord Dunraven?"

"Yes," Heart said softly.

"To the west they worry about Lord Irmaedith. East it's Lord Kaybale, to the south it's Lord Levin. But northward . . ."

Binney stopped midsentence.

Heart propped herself on one elbow, staring into the dark. "What's to the north, Binney?" she asked.

The Gypsy sighed. "Dunraven's Manor, of course, but past that, no one knows. There was a road once, people say. But if there was, Lord Dunraven has let the forest take it back."

Heart lay back down. "Will we go that way?"

Binney sighed. "No, child. No one does. Not for as long as I have lived, anyway."

✦ CHAPTER TEN

They spent the whole day getting ready. Heart kept glancing at the town girls who walked past.

Their skirts were perfect.

They wore little leather shoes without scuffs or mud on them.

Josepha caught Heart's eye. "They're jealous of us, you know," she whispered. "They get bored keeping clean." Beside Heart, Talia giggled.

Heart smiled at them both.

Men were shouting as the high wire was strung between two huge oak trees.

It was higher than Heart had ever seen it.

"Derrytown audiences see lots of Gypsies," Binney said. "It's harder to amaze them."

Heart walked around playing her flute, staying inside the circle of wagons.

Everyone was busy.

Davey was practicing his juggling.

Moonsilver and Avamir let her lean against them for a while. Then they moved away, restless.

When dusk finally came, Heart helped set up the lanterns in a circle. The townspeople started coming.

Whole families strolled down the streets. They paid their admission and found places to sit on the grass.

Heart had never *seen* so many people.

The show began with the Gypsy children singing, then doing flips across the grass.

When the people applauded, it sounded like thunder. Heart had goose bumps watching the performers.

Fiona and Sadie made the audience laugh out loud.

Josepha and Talia did their balancing act perfectly.

Heart was nervous. She glanced at Kip, sitting beside the unicorns.

Kip would do his part perfectly, she was sure. So would Moonsilver.

If she played her flute well . . .

Heart looked down at the silver flute. She fingered the keys, arching her hands the way Zim had taught her.

There was a round of applause and shouting.

Then another, even louder.

Heart looked up.

There, way up on the high wire, was Davey.

And he was *juggling*.

The heavy pins danced in a blurred circle between his hands.

The crowd gasped.

Davey took a step forward, walking the wire as he flipped the heavy clubs in a twirling circle.

Heart heard the audience draw in a breath. She held hers.

Davey was smiling. He walked in an even,

slow rhythm. He began to toss the heavy clubs higher and higher.

And then, suddenly, he lost his balance.

Heart stared. It was just a tiny loss of rhythm at first. Then he lurched to one side, bending sharply to recover.

But it was too late.

The audience went still as Davey plunged to the ground.

Binney screamed and ran toward him.

Heart found herself running too, her flute forgotten in her hand. The Gypsies formed a worried ring around Davey.

He wasn't moving.

"Davey? Davey!" Binney pleaded.

But he didn't move.

Heart could hear the audience murmuring.

She glanced at them. People were standing up, trying to see better.

The thudding clatter of hooves didn't make sense to Heart at first.

Then she heard the audience's murmuring

rise to a roar and she knew what had happened.

She turned to see Moonsilver galloping toward her.

Binney saw him too, and she stood.

The audience was pouring toward them.

"Stand back," Binney shouted. "Get out of the unicorn's way!"

Heart could only watch as Moonsilver came forward, his neck arched, his horn lowered.

He touched Davey gently, the tip of his horn crossing Davey's lips.

A wind, a song, the sound of the moon sighing rose into the air.

Then it was gone and Heart wasn't sure she had heard it at all.

She could hear the audience talking, though, their voices a tangle of pitches and rhythms.

And she could hear Binney weeping.

Then Moonsilver stepped back.

Davey opened his eyes and sat up.

Heart covered her mouth with one hand.

She heard a soft, astonished murmur and

turned to see hundreds of people standing in a loose circle. The audience had mixed with the Gypsies, and they stood, shoulder to shoulder, staring.

Davey didn't seem to notice them.

He put his arms around Moonsilver's neck.

It was Zim who stepped forward and bowed, sweeping his hand out toward Davey and Moonsilver.

"Ladies and gentlemen," he said loudly. "Please be seated."

The crowd moved back across the grass. They found their places and sat down.

✦ CHAPTER ELEVEN

A tense hush fell, and Heart helf her breath.

"We are delighted that you have enjoyed our play, *The Unicorn's Secret*," Zim said loudly.

Before the audience could applaud, he raised his flute to his lips.

His eyes caught Heart's, and she realized she was holding her flute as well.

She raised it and walked to stand beside him. Zim led off, playing the melody that Heart had used to train Kip.

Kip dashed up from out of nowhere.

He and Moonsilver fell into their usual act. Leaping and galloping, the unicorn circled the ring of lanterns. Then he pranced to a stop. And he bowed.

The audience applauded wildly, shouting and whistling.

"Good night!" Zim called, and all the Gypsies bowed.

Heart played one of her own melodies, a lively tune, to make people walk faster as they left.

Only once the green was empty of townspeople did she stop playing.

"Let's build our fire," Binney said. "And then we had better have a talk."

The Gypsies all nodded and set about changing their clothes and setting up camp for the night.

Heart found Davey. "Why did you do that? You scared your grandmother half to death. And me," she added.

Davey frowned. "I just thought I could," he said quietly. "Moonsilver saved my life. He's . . . real, isn't he?"

Heart nodded.

Binney was calling for everyone to sit down.

Heart and Davey walked toward the fire to join the circle.

The grass was damp with night dew.

"Thank you, Heart," Binney said softly. "And Moonsilver. Without you my Davey might not be alive."

The Gypsies nodded and smiled at Heart. Fiona winked.

Moonsilver was standing at the edge of the circle with Avamir. The mare shook her mane. The tiny bells tinkled in the soft night air.

Binney cleared her throat. "I want to give Heart a gift."

Heart shook her head, but Binney walked toward her, one hand out.

"These belonged to my mother. She was told that they were strands of hair from a unicorn's mane." Binney paused. "The Queen of the Unicorns."

The Gypsies leaned and stretched, trying to see.

Heart looked into Binney's eyes.

They hugged, hard. Then Binney released her and put three threads into her hand.

Heart stared at them.

They were silver, thick and round.

They were exactly like the thread Ruth had given her.

They were the same as the strands of thread from the blanket Simon had sold. Her blanket.

Heart felt the silver threads around her wrist begin to turn, and tighten.

She looked down and caught her breath. The new threads were weaving themselves into the circle!

In an instant there were no loose ends. The bracelet of uneven knots had become a finely woven silver lace.

Heart saw Binney's eyes widen, but she said nothing aloud. No one else was close enough to have seen. Heart lowered her hand and let her sleeve cover the silver bracelet.

"We all need supper," Zim called out.

A round of laughter rose into the warm night.

Heart ate, but she kept touching the bracelet.

It was magical.

It had to be.

Finally everyone started for bed.

As Heart rose to go to Binney's wagon, she saw flickering shadows along the edge of the green.

She heard a soft, rough voice, talking low.

" . . . a real unicorn. Didn't you see?" it demanded. "We have to tell someone!" There were murmurs of agreement.

Heart's stomach wrenched. She knew that voice! And Ruth had said Tibbs Renner was coming to Derrytown.

Heart's eyes stung with tears.

Tibbs had always tried to cause her trouble.

He would make sure the rumors flew.

And the whispers from Derrytown would reach important ears, no matter where the Gypsies went. Heart bit at her lip. Which of the lords would not want a unicorn?

Moonsilver would soon be hunted *every-where*. And if the Gypsies tried to help her, they would be in danger, too.

Heart blinked and wiped at her eyes.

She loved Binney and Zim and Davey. Fiona and Josepha and Talia were so nice she was starting to love them, too.

Heart crawled into her blankets and told Binney good night. Then she lay awake long enough for the stars to trace their way across half the sky.

Where could she go?

How could she save Moonsilver and Avamir from Dunraven and the other powerful lords?

Finally she slid into a tense sleep.

Her dreams were fierce.

She was running for her life in stark, treeless mountains. The massive boulders were white and gray, the colors of a full moon. She saw a mountaintop far ahead and knew it was safe—if she could reach it.

Heart woke breathing hard.

Was the dream real? It *felt* real.

Heart touched the silver bracelet on her wrist,

then sat up. She slipped out of the wagon into the darkness, taking her carry-sack with her.

If she left now, the Gypsies would be safe.

They wouldn't know where she had gone.

Moonsilver and Avamir woke silently. Kip stretched.

Heart knew she had to find the moon-colored mountains.

Every lord in every forest would soon be hunting for Moonsilver.

Avamir shook her mane and the Gypsy bells jingled.

Heart smiled.

Ruth would know why she left. And Binney would know she loved them all too much to put them in danger.

The moon rose as Heart led the way into the forest.

Avamir and Kip walked side by side.

Moonsilver stayed close.

Heart could feel his warm breath on her shoulder.

HEART'S ADVENTURES CONTINUE IN
THE MOUNTAINS OF THE MOON
COMING IN JULY 2002

*The Gypsies know Moonsilver is a real
unicorn now—and the people in Derrytown
will soon figure it out. Tibbs Renner will
see to that. It won't be long before Lord
Dunraven's men are searching. Now more
than ever, Heart needs a safe place,
a home.*

Heart led the way through the midnight forest.

The pine trees rose against a starry sky.

Moon shadows striped the rocky ground.

Kip trotted beside Avamir, his ears high, his tail raised like a flag.

Behind Heart, Moonsilver blew out a long, soft breath.

He touched her shoulder lightly with his muzzle.

Heart sighed, turning the silver bracelet on her wrist as she walked downhill.

How had the silver threads woven themselves together?

Was it magic?

A whisper of breeze touched the treetops. Heart looked up at the moon, then back at the rocky hillside. They had to hide. But where?

Where were the moon-colored mountains she had dreamed about? Were they real? What lord owned them?

Heart tried to remember what Binney had told her.

"To the west is Lord Irmaedith," Heart whispered to herself.

She knew nothing about Lord Irmaedith.

Was he cruel?

Worse than Lord Dunraven?

If the pale mountains were his, would he let her pass?

"And to the East, it's Lord Kaybale," Heart said aloud, repeating Binney's words to quiet the questions spinning in her thoughts.

She had never heard of him before, either.

A boulder took shape in the moonlit dusk ahead, rising out of the ground, as big as a farmer's house.

Heart led the unicorns around it.

Heart could hear Kip's quick, panting breath.

At least he was excited about this journey. No one else could be.

Ruth was probably heartbroken.

Heart's Gypsy friends would be sad.

Binney would be worried.

But she would probably be relieved, too, Heart knew.

She didn't want trouble for the Gypsies.

"And I am afraid," Heart breathed, touching the silver bracelet on her wrist once more.

The six silver threads had somehow woven themselves together like lace. And they tell the story of my life, Heart thought.

Two had come from the blanket she'd been wrapped in when Simon found her by the Blue River.

One was a gift from dear Ruth Oakes.

Three were from Binney in thanks for Moonsilver's saving Davey's life.

Binney had said hers were from the Queen of the Unicorns' mane.

Heart glanced at Avamir.

The white mare was beautiful, and her mane was long and silky. But it was white, not silver.

So maybe that part wasn't true?

Avamir tossed her head.

The tiny Gypsy bells in her mane jingled within the vast silence of the forest, then stilled.

Heart felt Moonsilver's muzzle against her back again, a quick, warm touch. She wished desperately that she knew what to do, where to go.

"Lord Kaybale," she said aloud, trying to break the panic-circle of her thoughts by repeating what Binney had told her. "Lord Kaybale is to the east."

Heart liked the rounded, strong sound of the name Kaybale.

It was plain and sturdy like everyday words—

like rainwater or hearthstone. But Lord Kaybale's lands lay somewhere to the east—far beyond Ash Grove.

Heart was afraid to go back that way.

Lord Dunraven would soon hear about Moonsilver's saving Davey.

He might send a thousand men to search the roads.

He would want a real unicorn.

"Where can we go?" Heart asked the sky.

Northward was Lord Dunraven's manor. Southward lay Lord Levin's lands, according to Binney.

North, south, east, west.

There was no reason to think any direction led to safety.

A rustling sound up the slope made Heart turn.

She caught her breath.

A vague shape was slipping in and out of the moon shadows.

Someone—or something—was following her.

Experience the Magic

When the battered mare Heart Trilby takes in presents her with a silvery white foal, Heart's life is transformed into one of danger, wonder, and miracles beyond her wildest imaginings. Read about Heart's thrilling quest in

THE UNICORN'S SECRET # ① :
Moonsilver
0-689-84269-4

THE UNICORN'S SECRET # ② :
The Silver Thread
0-689-84270-8

THE UNICORN'S SECRET # ④ :
The Mountains of the Moon
0-689-84272-4

ALADDIN PAPERBACKS
Simon & Schuster Children's Publishing Division • www.SimonSaysKids.com